Conversations with Extinct Animals

Conversations with Extinct Animals

Patrick Lawler

TUSCALOOSA

FC2 is an imprint of the University of Alabama Press

Inquiries about reproducing material from this work should be addressed to the University of Alabama Press

Book Design: Publications Unit, Department of English, Illinois State University; Director: Steve Halle, Production Assistant: Jalissa Jones
Cover design: Matthew Revert
Typeface: Adobe Jenson Pro and Akagi

Library of Congress Cataloging-in-Publication Data is available from the Library of Congress.
ISBN: 978-1-57366-211-6
E-ISBN: 978-1-57366-914-6

For Dylan and Juju,
Keep Dreaming!

The extinct animals are still looking for home
Their eyes full of cotton

Now they will
Never arrive
   —W.S. Merwin

 It wants to be buried
in wings.
   —Linda Tomol Pennisi

The end of the world has already occurred.
   —Timothy Morton

What kind of beast would turn its life into words?
   —Adrienne Rich

But even assuming all this to be true; yet, were it not
for the whiteness, you would not have that intensified
terror.
   —Herman Melville

TABLE OF CONTENTS

PART I

PART II

PART III

PART I

AUROCHS

In my dream, I am being chased. I started having this dream after Zach, my roommate, committed suicide. I'm not certain of the thing that is chasing me: my fear of death, my fascination with death—death itself?

In my dream, I am being erased.

I live in The Facility. I don't mean I work there or am a patient there. And I am definitely not a visitor. No. I *live* there. I'm not sure, but I believe there is a lake full of floating heads and a gazebo overflowing with bees. I don't mention this to most people for obvious reasons. Anyway, it is as if everyone is speaking in a foreign language that I don't have a clue how to deciphe: Stone (who asks us to call him Dr.), crazy Wick, Professor Turritopsis Dohrnil when he sends a text, and Ukombozi when she comes to visit.

Sometimes it is best to produce documents that no one will ever read. Like Marriage Licenses. Like Death Certificates. Just so you know, I put this "assignment" inside the Box. Wick has some great advice. I'm sorry if things get overly confusing—but that's what happens when you live inside The Facility.

This is my assignment. Or more accurately my response to the assignment from the Professor. I want to stress that I am not a patient or a client or even a regular student. More like a research student—a student of altered states of the mind when it happens to involve the delusional and disturbed. So why am I doing this? Really not sure—I've never been great at completing assignments. Wick says sometimes you've got to grab the aurochs by the horns.

I don't want to make a big deal out of it, but it is as if at one time I had tasted a road, and it was more like a laceration than a boot. That's P. A.'s influence on me—hyperbolic metaphor—schizophasia—crazy talk. Quantum Thinking. P. A. Trick says, "The forest grows at the edge of the heart." Wick shakes her head as Trick's words grow around a bee hole. Trick calls our Team Sessions a hive—"our own private Colony Collapse Disorder."

"Life is a constant revelation of the layers of lies," said the Professor. "Each day you excavate the levels of the lithosphere. Get inside the dust and dirt." U says that after Zach died, he started blogging; she says he mastered the language of the dead. "What does that mean?" I ask.

"You know, lots of misspellings and no punctuation." U says it is hypergraphia—the obsessive compulsion to write—the intense desire to put it all down on paper. Regardless of whether anyone can read it. Or even if you're dead.

The Facility is a huge white structure. When you are inside, you do not think it exists—but, when you are outside, it is all you can see.

At one of our Team Sessions, Stone (who asks us to call him Dr.), hands me a Box. "You should put all your fears in here," he says. I want to tell him the Box isn't big enough, but Wick says it is always best to pretend you don't understand what people are saying. As if they are speaking in Ukrainian and you can only listen in Swahili.

In the Box, I put the picture of an aurochs that had been hanging on the wall of the corridor of The Facility.

It looks enormous and lost—and on the verge of vanishing.

PANTOMIME IN A STRAITJACKET

Cups of sawdust in the sockets,
I live in a country full of amnesia where
people forget what they are afraid of.
This is what the world looks like:
withered and wonderful.
Everyone thought the walls were real
until the pantomimist stepped right
through his fingers.
I live in a house of stone where my coal
brain flickers.
I wear a smile like a snapped twig.
Birds crash into my mildewed wig.
I stand on the thinnest of ice
in the thinnest of weather.
Scar-crow, they call to me.
This is my fear:
I am a wick afraid of the fire.

SELF-PORTRAIT

After handing me a sheet of paper and crayons, Stone (you know what he asks us to call him) tells me I need to draw a self-portrait. "Draw what you think other people see when they look at you."

I think about the wall of Extinct Animals.

And then he says, "Look at the self-portrait you drew—and answer these questions:

What does this person dream?

What is he drowning in?

What is a secret this person has never told anyone?

Describe this person's favorite hiding place.

What is this person afraid of?

If this person were drowning, who would save him?

What does this person desire?

Who does this person love?

Would you give this person a stone to roll up a hill?

If this person were an Extinct Animal, what animal would it be?"

I think about the wall of Extinct Animals—and want to dissolve behind the colors and hide behind the melancholy eyes.

THE DODO

In The Facility, I am many rooms. Once I found a dead body, but I never told anyone. I asked Zach, what do you want. "What do you really want?"

Zach said he just wanted to sit in a rowboat in the middle of a lake, fishing when there are no fish. Just him and the rowboat—and the water.

Outside the windows, the birds move the sky with their shoulders. They go flap—but don't make a sound.

"Well, if you think you can do any better," I say to Stone (you know), "then why don't you live my life." And that's what is happening.

"Do you want to talk about it?" I ask Stone, who is living his life as me.

A terrible bird's shadow is as big as The Facility and swoops and caws like crazy—mythical and monstrous. Lunging and hungering.

It is as if it sucks all the air up with its breathing.

In The Facility, I hang around the pathetic one-shelf library with a row of self-help books: *How to Have at Least One Friend*; *Stop Being Who You Are*; *Don't Trust Anyone—Especially Your Inner Voice*.

When the Professor writes to me, his ideas go right to my brain before I have time to duck. "At what point do we invent the future?" he asks. I don't tell him I am afraid of clocks—how the sound gnaws at the heart, how the numbers crumble when the minute hand passes.

In the Team Session, P. A. Trick talks about sustainability sex. Trick calls it ecosex—where the energy expended is equal to the energy created. Wick says it sounds like a Beatles song.

We spend our lives travelling on streets that have been lost on maps—past tears, past pain, past love, past the voracious clocks. Yeah, the clocks. As the light gets old, it gets heavy. It crawls out of the morning—and slips back into the evening.

At first, I was afraid of the dead body—as if I were responsible for it. And then it just seemed obvious: at some visceral level Stone was responsible for it.

We sit in chairs opposite each other. Looking at the picture of the weird bird, Stone says, "I think one of us is losing it." And I don't say that I feel as if I were meant to be a fish in Zach's fishless lake.

FUNAMBULIST

The cages are made of barbed wire.
My roommate flew into death.
He flapped his arms over the dense
dark.
I learned from the lepidopterist
the flower is the gut of a butterfly.
When I started thinking about the thorn
pie, I had esophageal spasms.
There were glass shards in the crust.
That's life, said my roommate.
The scariest thing is
when you have to crawl
between two minds.

GREAT AUK

IN MY DREAM, I AM BEING CHASED. I started having this dream after Zach, my roommate, committed suicide. The thing that is chasing me: my fear of death, my fascination with death—and death itself.

Stone (who complains about everything) says I am repeating myself.

Maybe it's the guilt for being alive? Or my fear of Life? Maybe it is what I flee from and ironically what I try to save. It is the Twisted Man in a wire coat.

It is what all my words try to reveal. It is what all my words try to conceal.

Tangled anger. And untangled desire.

Stone says, "OK. OK."

"I wish you had introduced yourself before you tried to kill me." I wonder who is saying this. Stone. Or my roommate. Or Ukombozi—my roommate's former girlfriend. I always call her U. Which can get confusing.

The Twisted Wire Man who lives in the cellar. The I-am-afraid man. The I-am-not-afraid man.

"Please do not eat me," says the person who is dreaming this inside my head.

Why would anyone choose death? This is crazy. This is a

metaphor. This is crazy. Something half-buried like a spike in a tree hammered down deep. Something that is waiting to be born—a thorn tree growing in a womb.

In the Professor's text, he tells me you need to travel deep into the forest until you become a tree. He didn't say what kind of tree—and that is disturbing.

Wick tells me she once went with a man who wore black, and they made love on a pile of umbrellas.

Wick says she has a love for fallen things.

Everything is a metaphor. You know, the Professor's text and what Wick said. It is the very essence of metaphor because it is always something else.

The Twisted Wire Man. Always something—and something else. A dent. A piece of static. A crack. Shock waves. A shocked man. Off-kilter. Scraping his wires against the air, the Twisted Wire Man crackles when he walks. This is what my roommate looks like after he has died.

AT LEAST DEATH WAS DEPENDABLE

Wick is a part of the Team Session.
She writes her name all over the surface
of her skin. She says the child lives in a
book; she says the dead man
resides in her head.
The eye I was given is turning around
in its socket to look into the woods
where the gravestones genuflect.
I keep digging into stars.
When the obituary writer dies,
there is no one left to say it,
and, because there is no one left
to say it, it never happens.
Immortality.
When collaborating with the dead,
sell little packets of nostalgia—
gouge out the darkness where the dead

used to sit.

The tombstone carver is the one with the blank stone.

STELLER'S SEA COW

I BELIEVE I'VE HEARD THIS BEFORE—but I live in The Facility. I don't mean I work there or I am a visitor or a patient there. No. I live there—deep in the penetralia where I have taken up residence. "Everybody's got to find their place in life," Stone tells me. And I say, "Mine just happens to be here. Among the movieheads."

I was a student in a Community College Writing Class, and for an assignment we were asked to do an ethnographic study.

I started with this: The Facility is like a great chunk of white polished Nothingness. A monolith with no meaning connected to it. A loneliness colossally present in its ghostliness. Like smoke from a tailpipe. There and not there.

"Tell me about yourself," they always say. Salesperson. Engineer. IT. HR.

Movieheads is what I call them. They just live inside different movies—and they take pills that help them to rip up the scripts.

P. A. Trick is part of the Team Session. He says, "Call me P. A. Trick. Not my real name, of course. But then who among us goes by real names anymore." P. A. Trick says everything is in a name. "I'm more trick than pa."

Looking at the pictures of the Extinct Animals, I can't help but wonder if it is too late to save the world—especially since there are so many different worlds. In the Nondenominational Chapel, the saints gather: St. Television, St. Pandemic, St. Dymphna, St. Sisyphus, St. Zarathustra.

Wick tells me she once had sex with a depressed photographer on a pile of negatives.

In the middle of the Team Session, suddenly I realize I have nothing left to talk about. "I've said all I have to say," I say to Stone. I've heard all I've had to hear. And the person who asks us to call him Dr. says he's heard it all before.

Obviously, we're running out of tunnel, and pretty soon all there will be is light—as ominous as that sounds.

The Facility is a lockbox full of desires and diagnoses, full of magic and madnesses, mirages and amnesia. Luckily, the key is locked inside.

Let's face it, I have a burned brain. I imagine P. A. Trick wearing a mud-brown hood—reciting the alphabet in a Gregorian hum. I believe The Facility is a hostel for time travelers with backpacks and vape pens. St. Omnicide staggers out of the future.

It is impossible for me to forget the pictures on the walls—all the Extinct Animals arranged chronologically by the dates when each of them perished.

Staring out of the emptiness with their exquisitely vacant eyes.

WEARING MASKS

I sit with a Doctor. I am wearing
a mask. He is wearing a mask.
The Doctor is wearing a Sigmund Freud
mask. I am wearing a Carl Jung mask.
I am wearing the mask with a tear
soldered to the cheek.
The Doctor wears my father's mask.
I am wearing his father's mask.
We don't recognize each other.
The Doctor starts drawing on my mask.
The Doctor and I exchange masks.
The masks start kissing.
Ugh, says one of the masks.
We are happy that there are no
eyeholes in the mask.

LABRADOR DUCK

"You have a visitor." I always hate these words. It reminds me too much of what is out there. It is as if someone is saying: here is your past—right in front of you. Here is a present that you have no control over. What did you think "now" looks like?

I look at the elevator door where everything arrives and leaves. It is like a vertically mobile metaphor. Like a slow-moving Time Machine.

"Look," Ukombozi says, "It's been tough for everyone. Zach was great—but you've got to pull yourself together. You don't have a special claim on grief, you know."

She adjusts her attitude in the orange plastic chair.

"You know the problem with white people?" she asks.

"Kinda," I say.

"You feel you shouldn't have to think about death—that you shouldn't ever have to be sad, that you are entitled to be happy every day of your petty life. Well, guess what?"

I pick at the armrest on my beige plastic chair and dig at the beige blisters. I feel the indentations with my forefinger.

"You build everything around the fact that you are sup-posed to be happy—malls and amusement parks and sitcoms and stupid golf courses and the whole goddamn pharmaceutical industry."

I call her U—but sometimes that gets confusing. Eventually U leaves.

One day you're here doing whatever shit you are required to do to create a here—and then the next moment there is another here—unrecognizable and disruptingly different. Scary even. New things are in this new here. Old things are missing. Whatever you feel about it doesn't really matter. Whatever it looks like—vivid or blurred—you know another here is on its way to replace it.

Just like that. And the elevator door opens.

OPENING UP

LABRADOR DUCK

I'm full of contradictions—mainly
because I have too many people
residing in me. If one of them died,
I'd still have dozens
to attend the funeral. We do not look
like our descriptions. Actors really don't
know what they look like,
so they try to catch themselves
when they're not looking.
Some losses cannot be compensated
for—only dimly grasped.
I began by mimicking what I was losing.
The process was instructive.
I ended by mimicking what I was loving.
That's when everything
still existed as stars.

PÈRE DAVID'S DEER

Wick asks, "Why would you walk around with a Box?"

Here's what I want to know: why would somebody kill himself? I know the Camus book. I had to read it for my philosophy course at the local community college. Not that I finished it. Then again, if you committed suicide, you didn't finish life. So maybe I'm not an expert—but still I've got the experience of witnessing what isn't finished. Now that I think of it, the Professor of the course gave me an incomplete.

When we sit in the Team Session, P. A. Trick hums "Dark Side of the Moon."

Stone (remember?) asks me, "Why are you stealing the pictures of the Extinct Animals?"

Before Philosophy Class, Zach handed me a book, and I turned it over—*The Myth of Sisyphus*. It was ratty and torn—as if had been chewed on endlessly. It was a book that looked like it had killed itself—and had good reason to do it.

U asks, "Why can't you move on?"

I ask her, "How could *you* have possibly moved on?"

"Let's face it," she says, "You were only his roommate."

"And you were his *only girlfriend*," I say.

Professor Turritopsis Dohrnil asks, "Have you read the book yet?"

The world becomes the precise shape of each of the Professor's words—crumbly clouds. Will time become extinct—and then will we all exist in a perpetual Now—and everything around us will be mud? I have to stop reading the Professor's texts.

In the Team Session, Wick says she is an "astro-naught." "Not astronaut. Astro-naught. A navigator of Nothingness."

P. A. Trick hums "Space Oddity."

At first, I began writing this in one of the extinct languages—Eyak or Yana or Susquehannock. And then I decided to write it in a future extinct language.

Wick says the Box thing is just weird. She asks, "Who's that a picture of?"

I tell her I don't know—and intend to leave it at that. She asks if he is swimming or drowning—and I shrug my shoulders as if I'm doing both.

LIFTING WITH A PITCH-FORK A PIECE OF LIGHT

There is a proliferation of thinking
things as if the whole world
were strangled in violin strings—
always with a profusion of bruises
and blossoms. I need to feed the blind
with spoonfuls of light.
One day a flower blossoms backward
into dirt. Across the sky, we push
a constellation with a broom.
The rocks are shaped into clouds.
I need to operate a CRISPR, so I can edit
DNA and bring everything back to life.
When I look out the one Facility
window, I see the stars stab their way
through the darkness and the window
bars.

PASSENGER PIGEON

In the Ghost Lounge, they just sit staring out at the Empty. The Empty just comes and sits down next to us. Hey, it says. The TV hums.

TV signals are flying through the cosmos at the speed of light. More than four hundred trillion miles from Earth. Hard to calculate the Neilsen ratings.

Somebody is sitting down light years away in a galactic plastic living room . . . watching *Howdy Doody* and *The Twilight Zone* and *The Brady Bunch* and *Star Trek*.

I wanted to accumulate the raw material of everything in order to regrow the world. Bullfrogs and alpine plants and berries— and all the things that grew behind the screen.

When I will be an old man, I will lose my son. When I was a child, I lost my grandfather. But it was OK because it was in a mall, so he could just wander for decades among the labyrinth of things.

Once I bought a generator—just in case. I'm not sure what is going to happen—but I will be ready for it. I've learned this: conservatives buy guns. And liberals buy generators. Both eventually go bang.

I need more wick than wax. And I'm not thinking of Wick. She says she has discovered a hole behind the TV in the Ghost Lounge. She tells me she entered it and found a room inside.

Stone says: Time feels all wounds. Or something like that.

He says, "You need to acknowledge what has happened."

I don't need a generator to know that how a person commits suicide is a statement—one that needs to be interpreted and analyzed. So, I keep thinking about Zach.

I ask Wick, "So, why do you walk around with a mirror?" She explains that Stone asks her to do it, so she can see her real self.

And then she shows it to me, and it's totally empty. "I broke it," she says. "And then they took away the shards, so the real self wouldn't use them to get at the real me."

When I sit staring out at the Empty in front of the empty TV, I think about the broken mirror.

TAKING A TRAIN TO CRAZY TOWN

"You think you're special—but you are
nobody,"
I can feel the craziness crawling
on my neck. Let me draw you
a picture—my photo-sin-thesis—
about free-floating connectivity.
I live on borders. How is life
threatening you? In the surge
and spiraling of our relationship,
she was my soulbird.
The chemicals of our blessings
get all over us. Death puts its dark
gift on our doorstep. It is irresistible.
It needs to be opened . . . and
opened . . . and opened.

CAROLINE PARAKEET

"WHAT KIND OF A NAME IS WICK?" I say. But she doesn't answer. She just looks at the group with disdain, with a kind of existential deconstructionism. It is as if I weren't an individual but had somehow become the whole group.

"What the fuck?" she says.

Later I ask, "How did you get here?"

"Brain fire," Wick says. "I'm here for the promotions."

We live inside a perpetually voracious animal. This is what I'm thinking.

Stone says look inside the Box.

Later Wick says to me, "I used to stand in front of the rack of cards in the drugstore. And I imagined I received the birthday cards and holiday cards and the sorry cards. I imagined the people who sent them to me."

"Even the get-well cards?" I ask.

Wick says, "In the total realm of it all, we are dust balls." I don't think she is talking directly to me. Still, I admire her deconstructionist existentialism.

In my psychological experiment conducted for Professor Turritopsis Dohrnil's class, I intend to disclose the character of those willing to take part in psychological experiments. The results: Those who take part fall into two groups: inveterate liars and people who only want to please others. Thus, the results are always false. Always.

How did we get here? It is like we live inside a subway without the trains, without the destinations, without the tracks. And the lights are blinking and eventually go out. And we are moving faster and faster. And faster. Choking on huge bits of darkness as we go.

I sometimes feel the immense hunger of The Facility. I hear it chewing on the heart. I hear it swallowing the brain. I hear it crunching on the soul.

"So, you're here because your roommate committed suicide? Do they have cards for that?"

I wonder which group I would be a part of.

"Dust ball," Wick says. "That's what I'd put inside your Box."

THIS IS THE WAY THE WORLD BEGINS

CAROLINA PARROT.—*Conurus carolinensis.*

The trees remember everything,
and those memories become our
houses. I grab butterflies out of the air
and feel the tiny bones in their wings.
A diagram for beauty is in the butterfly's
brain. We record heartbeats.
I'm trying to stay only one person.
The carpenter builds his body into the
house. Perhaps I will die from an
overabundance of joy.
We build houses in the trees—
mansions in our hearts.
Our eye weighs as much as the world.

PART II

THYLACINE

PROFESSOR TURRITOPSIS DOHRNIL SENDS ME MAIL. I suspect someone from the Research Team screens everything. I'm hoping for something that will inspire me.

"How is the research going?" he asks.

Zach was writing something he called "Cartographies of Madness." It was for an Independent Study with the Professor. I suspect the Professor is sending me pieces of Zach's writing—little disjointed fragments intended to eventually become a whole.

All his classes explained different dimensions of the real. The Professor of Paradox, the Professor of Everything—the Professor of Quantum Taxonomy. He explained Reality, its murkiness. Its entangled fluidity. We believe it is either all words or all numbers, he said. And then he provided a formula and then a whole new alphabet. The students knew he was either a genius or a crazy genius.

To explain Reality, we went from math to words. Big mistake. Then we went from words to silence—monastic characters seeking our spiritual cleansing.

We are just particles existing in multiple places simultaneously both alive and dead—eating from Schrödinger's cat dish. Yumyum. Licklick.

We rub against each other's perceptions.

P. A. Trick says he has a thousand different costumes. "A thousand different disguises." He says he has a bonnet full of bees; he says I'm crazy. Oh, man.

Zach used to say it was his goal to go back in time to save one Extinct Animal. U would shake her head.

Human observations determine the reality we perceive. But suppose "human observation" is an illusion—that we are the ones being observed by a presence that is both alive and dead. "Did you ever play three thousand–card monte?" the Professor asks. "That's reality."

We are numbers and words and silence. Simultaneously.

And we maneuver along with the Extinct Animals beside the cat's dish—each of us both alive and dead.

Wick says, "Let me show you the hole behind the TV."

THE HOUSE WON'T LET US DIE

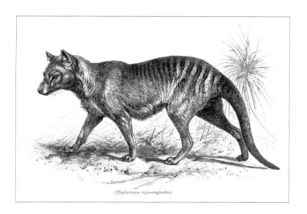

(Thylacinus cynocephalus)

At first, everyone thinks they are
miracles—individual, unique miracles.
And then they think they are mistakes.
At first, they are dazzled and then they
are angry. The paranoid schizophrenic
becomes afraid of hands.
When the magician goes inside a hat,
he finds clouds. Tiny mice
with dandruff are as fine as felt dust.
When he goes inside his hat,
the magician finds a little fire—
the remnants of thought: smoke.
The paranoid schizophrenic starts eating
her memories until she is empty.

MIND MAP

Stone (the Dr.) says I should draw a map of how I think.

He says, "This will help you to clarify your thoughts—and perhaps you will be able to find alternative routes."

He wants me to create a wiring diagram of all one hundred trillion connections between the neurons of the human brain.

Here is what he tells me:

> Create your connectome.
>
> Imagine you had the brain of a goldfish. Would you be a better swimmer?
>
> Determine how fast a thought travels. And then slow it down, so you can look at it.
>
> There are as many stars in our galaxy as neurons in the human brain. Think about it. And then explode.
>
> Look up at the sky at night—and look directly at your brain.

After looking at what I had done, he holds the intricacies and mysteries of my mind in his hands. He examines the inscrutable circles, traces with his finger the webwork of lines, and rubs his thumb over the smudge marks. He says, "OK. Maybe we should approach this differently."

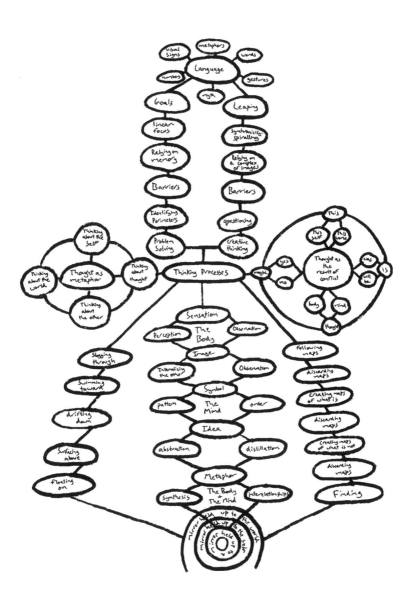

BALI TIGER

"Don't you even feel guilty?" I say to U.

From across the table, she looks past me.

"You know? Guilty about Zach. Maybe, if you hadn't broken up with him," I say—and then I feel kind of sorry for saying it.

I think of my grandmother—the more she descended into the crumpled world of Alzheimer's, the luckier she got. We'd bring her scratch tickets and watch her win. In the end she never lost. There were all these dark crumbs around her fingers. And she kept winning and winning.

I've been thinking lately. Suppose he was killed, and it was cleverly made to look like suicide. Or maybe he was talked into suicide in a very subtle manner, believing it was his own free will—while in reality he was being nefariously manipulated.

Wick says, "If you ever looked closely at a fly—I mean really closely, examining its vibrant being, how could you kill it? In a square mile there are thirty-six million insects. An ocean of compound eyed beings live around us. How could anybody kill even one?"

Stone says, "I don't know what you look like until I see your mask." Makes sense.

And then I think about my grandmother. How weird it was. The more she descended into darkness, the luckier she got.

Eventually, a golden road stretched directly out of her heart, and she walked down it into her death. Maybe Zach felt that way.

"You know you have to acknowledge the fact that you are not merely pretending you are insane in order to complete your research. You are not putting 'an antic disposition on,'" says U. "You have definitely tipped over the edge."

"What are you looking at?" I ask.

She points to one of the Extinct Animals. "Look at it. It's beautiful. So incredibly beautiful," she says. "And gone. As if one day, it walked off down a road—and never came back."

We sit silent a long time—and then she stares directly at me. "Maybe that's what it takes to reach the pinnacle of our own beauty."

I AM BEING SHAPED BY A WHOLE SERIES OF FAKE MEMORIES

I need to find a map that will show me
how to get out of here—but always
there is the tie that blinds.
I heard them say: Listen for the lifeboats
'til it hurts. Overdose on light
at an exponential rate.
Clouds are sliced on the windmill's
blades. There is an intruder
under my skin. I need to weed the
soul—calamitous, necrotic, punctured.
There are tiny bursts of memory.
The right eye touches what the left eye
sees. Windows rinsed with tears.
A world falls beneath the shadows.
Is it necessary for me to say I am being
squashed inside a flower?

SCHOMBURGK'S DEER

Code Blue means one thing, and Code White means something else.

I feel I have to know this, just in case.

Sometimes I hear these cryptic messages come over the intercom in The Facility.

Code Pink must mean something.

We are in the dining area, and P. A. Trick appears to say foreign words to a bowl of strawberries: "*To glyko mouni sou.*"

Wick says that some of the residents when they get special permission can go in the courtyard. And some of them have sex in the gazebo. The staff calls it Code Red because of all the red rosebushes that grow around the gazebo. There are also a hundred bees.

At first, I thought the Professor said immoral jellyfish—instead of the "Immortal" Jellyfish. He said, call me Professor Turritopsis Dohrnil.

I tried on majors to see how they fit: Philosophy. Psychology. Literature. Theater. Ecology.

Nothing fit. Or maybe everything fit.

The Professor was involved in every one of my majors. He called it Quantum Entanglement. He called it Existential Deconstructivist Eclecticism.

He called it Brainability.

He says everything depends on how much we can forget.

"Nobody is who you think they are," says U the next time she visits.

I have learned the more beautiful the name the more deadly the disease. It gives you something to strive for.

Wick says she once went with a PhD student, and they made love on a pile of quotes.

I think I'd like to make love on a pile of clocks—until the second hand crumbles up the numbers.

Over the intercom, Code Red crackles.

THE PARABLE HIDES INSIDE A RIDDLE

HEAD OF SCHOMBURGK'S DEER.
(From Sclater, *Proc. Zool. Soc.*, 1877.)

If you have Jerusalem Syndrome,
you believe you are Jesus or Mary Mag-
dalene or Peter or Judas.
I carry around a parable just in case.
Fish hide inside the water; the water
hides inside the river. The river hides
inside the sea; the sea hides inside the
fish.
Before I can imagine owning a boat,
I buy an oar just to get used to the
idea. I lug it around on my back.
Just in case the opportunity arises,
I carry a small bag of silver.

TOOLACHE WALLABY

Suddenly, I become obsessed with the weight of things. A song. A pen. An apostrophe.

How much does reality weigh? What is the weight of a black hole? White hole?

Everything is just a little bit crazy. And what does crazy weigh?

Here is how I would determine the weight of the soul. I would weigh Zach just before he killed himself. And then weigh him right after. The difference would equal the weight of the soul. It makes sense.

That's when things start breathing.

Sometimes Wick won't stop talking: "I would always stop the car and get out just in case I'd run over anyone. The sky looks like Windex. People wearing ski masks come away with duffel bags. No one is certain what is inside them—though it doesn't sound like bones. Authorities say nothing is unnatural. My search engine goes looking for God. Everything goes back to its origins. Hydrogen separates from oxygen. A bee listens. My consciousness is slipping. Jesus looks like Woody Allen. In Argentina, one general loaded all the homeless on a bus and sent them someplace else. Snowflakes fall out of the stars. I knew I was too skinny when the automatic doors wouldn't slide open for me anymore."

When I see her again, U warns me about Wick. "You don't really know her."

Wick says she loves Emily Dickinson. "Each of her poems swallows little bits of me. You know, you cannot put a fire out. That's so true."

P.A. Trick belongs to the Magicians Union—they made the apostrophe disappear. He says Nijinsky intended to patent a new type of pen under the brand name "God."

Wick says the most loving thing you can do after you are dead is to mix your ashes with the one you love.

A song is left behind in a birdcage. A song plays in the background: "Don't Rain on my Charade."

Wick says we are too much human and not enough being.

U hasn't been to see me in weeks, so who is she to warn me about anybody?

When she finally comes to visit me, she has a pen in her hand and says that nobody is who you think they are.

THE TRAFFIC LIGHT
BLINKING UNDERWATER

WHALLABEE.—*Halmaturus ualabatu.*

Because the river flooded the rich
people's houses, they insisted a dam
be built with a man-made lake behind it.
Men came and said they had to drown
our town. The bridge sunk
underwater—and the train tracks.
The cemeteries and the churches
with Jesus gasping for air. The sunken
library with waterlogged books.
People in scuba masks floated in
and out of the underwater shops.
The mental hospital flooded.
Hallucinations strapped to scuba tanks
drifted to the surface.

BARBARY LION

STONE SAYS I SHOULD WRITE A LETTER TO ZACH.

> *Dear Zach,*
>
> *OK. I don't really know what I'm writing. Call this an elegy, a testament, an exorcism.*
>
> *I'm not in any hurry to let you know what I'm feeling.*

Wick says, "On YouTube you can talk to the dead."

I discover the inner parts of The Facility. The sanctum sanctorum.

The penetralia.

My roommate was always trying to commit suicide. I'd come back from class—and there he'd be hanging around. Sorry. Bad joke.

> *Dear Zach,*
>
> *Here are some things I wish we had talked about:*
>
> *1.*
>
> *2.*
>
> *3.*

I discover the inner space of The Facility: the Qumran Cave, the Nectary.

You can always tell the ones who've been out to the gazebo because when they come back in The Facility they have all these beestings.

The secret space is behind the elevator door. People come in with passes stuck to their lapels. The door opens and U comes in as if she has been living behind that door for weeks.

> Dear Zach,
>
> How are your plans going for your digital afterlife?
>
> I wish you hadn't died.

THANK-YOU NOTE FROM A MANNEQUIN

I was raised on a mannequin farm
where everyone seemed kind of real.
Convulsively, the road erodes beneath
us. Once I played a piano on top
of a dump. I used to send out thank-you
notes after a) sex b) therapy c) recitals.
If you have Koro Syndrome, you believe
your penis has been stolen. Thank you.
The hebephrenic laughs her heart off.
The great thing is mannequins
don't urinate.

CARIBBEAN MONK SEAL

Wick keeps a fake diary.

> Day 1: I fear I am inside a creature—and all of us are fed time until we are bursting.

> Day 2: It's like I'm a bird in a barbed wire cage.

So why am I studying The Facility? The human propensity to discover meaning infuses life. Or so my professor says. I just want to be able to see things—differently.

> Day 3: I'm looking for life at the end of the tunnel.

> Day 4: I must mean light?

We are so obsessed with our psychological world we forget the world we are losing.

P. A. Trick says we are flailing. He says The Facility swallows all meaning.

I say to U, "You don't know anything?"

And she says, "The difference between me and you is that one day in the future I *will know* everything." Acolytes cryptically carry light inside things.

Zach told me when he would read he turned into the

characters he was reading about—and this is why he didn't read the bible. "Hamlet. Gregor Samsa.

Emma Bovary. Quentin Compson. But no biblical characters."

> DAY 5: I have a dream where Rudolf Steiner talks about the unconscious wisdom of the hive.

I tell U, "Here are some things I do:"
I do a dance and deliver a soliloquy on a dead stump.
I fish in the amygdala.

> DAY 6: I learn not to forge my signature on suicide notes.

> DAY 7: Light is dumped all over my inner being.

> DAY 8: I am reading John Wheeler's theory about a participatory universe.

> DAY 9: I am starting to sleep with monsters. I am starving to sleep with monsters.

> DAY 10: I write my fake diary.

A SORCERESS IN THE CRAZY PLACE

Even among the tantalizingly elliptical,
I remain in the grip of forgetfulness.
Honey or pus. I'm never really sure
which I'm addicted to.
Still, I keep telling myself: Don't be
afraid. We are all part of a shaken-up
world. I belong to a tribe that believes in
desire. We are all part of a shake-down
world. I belong to a tribe that believes it
has disappeared. And all the while the
bees teach us to dance.

CASPIAN TIGER

WE ARE EVERYONE. And each of our jobs is to make people think we aren't all of us—but of course that is not true. So, we become fearful of our intimate connections with everything around us—and then we start building walls out of our own identities.

Wick says she needs to have a conversation with the others within.

"Don't be one of those people who leave their souls behind the walls of The Facility," says U. U tells me about the places that propagate people behind their walls. St. Remy grows Van Gogh; Nietzsche talks to God in Basel; and Nijinsky spin-dances with angels in Switzerland's Bellevue.

Ezra Pound wobbles on the holy ground of St. Elizabeth's. Allen Ginsberg first hears the howl in his mother's room in the Pilgrim Psychiatric Center. Frederick Law Olmsted designs the grounds at the McLean Hospital where he eventually becomes a patient—and where Sylvia Plath closes her eyes and the world drops dead. While Robert Lowell is in Boston Psychopathic Hospital, Anne Sexton listens to God's brown goodbye voice on the Bedlam lawn.

I think they are all members of the Extinct Animal Club—and U is the President.

Stone's dreams are weird. When the Box gets filled, I start another one.

I sit in front of him—confused by his apparitional presence. I step into fog.

The Facility is dedicated to taking us out or taking us in. The Facility is a Ful-filiament Center—stuffed with plastic gratitude and scratchy light. It is a hyperobject—a twenty-eight-dimensional knot that we are inside entangled in string and dangly theory.

P. A. Trick says, "I am in the miracle business. We put our loves together the way someone might write a book." Trick is in the library.

The Facility is a hive with a hive brain and a leader with borderline personality disorder. The workers are involved in the production of Einstein umbrellas that require a gnostic formula to open.

Wick says, "I used to want to have sex with a firefly." My problem was that I had too little sex.

Wick says everything I thought I made up turned out to be real. And vice versa.

I write eulogies for the living with a relentless receptivity and soulfulness. My occupation should have been a fake-sex choreographer for TV. Move a little to the right, I'd advise.

That's not the way it's done, I'd admonish. My problem was that I had too much sex—granted it was fake-TV sex. I discover a different kind of gravity. A special kind of grace.

Wick shows me a book, *The Complete Poems of Emily Dickinson.* "Really? Where did you find it?"

"In the library." "You mean with the twenty self-help books and a dictionary? Seems crazy." She tells me in a former life, she used to be Emily Dickinson. I ask her if she believes in reincarnation, and she says, "No, but just because I don't believe in something, doesn't mean it isn't true."

I ask U where she learned all that stuff about mental hospitals. "Zach," she answers.

MY FATHER USED TO BURN DOWN THE HOUSE REGULARLY

People came with ladders and leaned
them against the burning windows;
some came with hacksaws
to cut through the candles.
America is on fire.
Pica is compulsion to eat nonnutritive
materials—like chalk or dirt or soap.
Like the fire inside America.
I want to eat the apocalypse.
Sleep sews my soul inside a sack.
The clock sucks up the past around it.
The next thing to happen wonders why
it didn't happen earlier.

SOCORRO DOVE

IF YOU HAVE COTARD'S SYNDROME, you believe you are already dead. Death arrives in a bowler hat—a nice-enough chap with a pack of cards and an elegant invitation.

I have learned that everything has a memory. The train first arrives in the suitcase. Sinkholes are the way the earth has of swallowing itself up—the dirt creating its own black hole.

Wick grew up in a town where there were more churches than people. She says, "It is sometimes best to think of people as shadows." I grew up in a town with more bars than people—where everyone really was a shadow.

U says we have an unquenchable desire to be part of others—to peer through a microscope into the soul of a neighbor.

U tells me she has discovered posted in The Facility's elevator a LIST OF EXPERIMENTS:

> The Milgram Experiment
>
> The Stanford Prison Experiment
>
> Missing Child Experiment
>
> Harlow's Monkeys Experiment
>
> I Lost my Mime over Her Experiment

Wick tells me we are part of the Gazebo Experiment, the Box

Experiment. The Hole Experiment, the One-Thousand-Suitcases Experiment.

I peer into all the painful silent contortions of what it is to be human. P. A. Trick says, "What do you think, I'm a mime reader?"

He is always cape-swirling; he says the part of truth he most admires is the part he has to make up. His fingers maneuver elegantly around a deck of unopened cards.

I have come to realize the universe is no more than the size of a word. And it sits snuggly in the Dictionary in the library.

When I look at the pictures on the walls, I see the light that is swallowed and disappears around the bodies of the Extinct Animals.

Stone tells me there is a diagnosis—but he isn't going to tell me. However, he does say we need to focus on apophatic vectors of energy.

Wick takes me behind the TV in the Ghost Lounge. She takes me inside the hole. I look around. "What are all these boxes?" I ask. "One thousand suitcases," she says.

A REAL DANCER

A real dancer dances until her legs
break. Unless you kill the monster,
you become the monster—
but then in killing the monster,
of course, you become . . . never mind.
I carry a bag of bones, a bag of souls, a
bag of words while I watch a bird darkly
scissoring its way through the sky.
And, of course, the goddess
who is protected by birds has seen a lot
of homes fall into the ocean.
The real dancer dances until her feet
catch fire, until her ankles snap,
until her heart bursts.

PART III

JAPANESE SEA LION

"I'VE DISCOVERED A PRIMITIVE TRIBE that lives in the basement," Wick says with a sense of urgency. "They call themselves the Dream Dwellers." We are sitting in the twenty-one-book library.

She tells me they believe they die every night in their dreams, and, in the morning, they are reborn—thus, they are immortal. As long as they wake up.

"Still, they carry substantial life insurance. Just in case," Wick says.

At night diminishing and disappearing, and in the morning erupting and flowing.

They have no need for a word for *want* in their language.

Wick says I should write down my desires on a list and dig a hole. "Place the list inside a hole and bury it."

"Then what?" I ask. "Nothing really," says Wick. "It just is a nice place to keep your list."

I suppose I should tell you about Wick's hair. Sometimes it is pink or orange or purple. Her hair color isn't determined by artificial dyes but rather melanocytes and amino acids that far exceed the range of the typical hair color on the Fischer-Saller scale. Rather the color of her hair seems to spontaneously select itself from a palette of pigments resembling paint charts in a hardware store. Over the months, I discovered her hair color is related to the codes that come over the intercom.

P. A. Trick says our one-shelf library needs its own shelf-help book.

Trick says there's a music box inside his head with a song played on lobotomy ice picks and astral talismans. The chanteuse must always be mortally wounded so death flows out of the mouth.

The Facility begins to take on a life of its own. It throbs with a kind of electricity. A pulse. Of course, it started out with an immense hunger.

Wick tells me she was passionate with an Extinct Woman whose name meant Redemption, and they made love on the backs of lions—a Barbary lion and a Japanese sea lion.

She says she knows objects around the bed gather the sleeper's breath as she sleeps. She says it is all about Transformation.

Once, Zach said we keep trying to teach the dead a lesson, but the dead don't stay in the places we put them. There is a frost the dead wear in their eyes—and he has to keep dying until he gets it right. He says the voice box is the size of a cricket—and I can barely hear him.

I read in his notebook: What does a mountain think of God?

Wick says you will know the Dream Dwellers are there because when you are scared, *I mean scared to death*, they will make a noise to let you know of their presence. And that should make you feel very afraid—and somehow hopeful.

When she tells me this, her hair is yellow.

ANGEL OF REDEMPTION

SEA LION.—*Otaria jubata.*

Suppose I am skydiving at the
moment of the apocalypse—and I think
maybe I've survived as I drift over the
burning lakes and the bony woods—
the smoking malls.
Then people come running to look up
to me, thinking I am an angel
who has come to save them.
Like I'm an Angel of Redemption.
As I approach the Earth, I try to figure
out something to say—
something that is hopeful and
entertaining, something that is brilliant
and at the same time emotional and
detached, as I descend toward the
scorched shore of the burning lake.
As I descend toward their shopping
carts and their outstretched souls . . .

A THOUSAND SUITCASES

STONE SAYS, "When the state mental hospital closed fifty years ago, workers discovered a thousand suitcases in the attic. I want you to find your suitcase among that thousand.

"The suitcases are filled with aspirations and accomplishments—stuffed with where they had been and where they were afraid to be going.

"The thousand suitcases are about loss and isolation and fear and sadness—but also strangely about hope."

"I don't get it," I say. "What does any of this have to do with me? Mental hospital? Suitcases? Fifty years ago? Fifty years ago I wasn't even me."

I learned the suitcases contained straggly underwear, dirty hats, torn shirts. Pictures of children. They contained Bibles and maps. Children's books and crumpled bits of tissue. Pictures of old people. A ukulele. A spoon. One rosary bead. A broken necklace. Wedding pictures. A squashed bonnet. Something that was gray like melancholia. Pictures. Pictures. Pictures.

"It's better than carrying around your dead grandparents," says Stone. "Better than carrying around your dead roommate."

He wants to know what would be in my suitcase.

"Make a list," he says.

RAINPLOPS

GLOSSOLALIA

NECTAR

A SELF-HELP BOOK

A FAKE DIARY

PICTURES OF EXTINCT ANIMALS

AN APOCALYPTIC TOY PIANO AND A RADIOACTIVE
UKULELE

POTTER FLOWER BEE

WICK'S BROKEN MIRROR

A CLIP FROM *STAR TREK* (THE ONE WHERE THEY DIS-
COVER A NEW PLANET)

ONE OF WICK'S GREETING CARDS

A TORN COPY OF *THE MYTH OF SYSYPHUS*

A DAMAGED EIGHT-TRACK TAPE WITH THE TITLE
"SOULILOQUE"

A DICTIONARY OF AN EXTINCT LANGUAGE

A SONG INSIDE AN EMPTY BIRDCAGE

PICTURES   PICTURES   PICTURES

WYOMING TOAD

TIME MOVES IN MUD down the hallways where the eyes of the dead stare. In the Ghost Lounge there is the altar of extinction. The athanor lives behind the elevator doors. From the Nondenominational Chapel, Lazarus comes out of the mushiness of death, mole like, adjusting his mask. The sky taps against the window.

Suppose the Extinct Animals didn't live on the walls. Suppose there are pictures of tantric poses. Pictures of bioluminescent deep-sea fish. Suppose there is a psychedelic hallucinatory blaze. Beautiful and scary and beautiful. How would everybody be different if the pictures that grew on the walls told a different story?

I feel the cells in my amygdala responding to the pictures of the Extinct Animals.

My father once said, "I only drink when I get overwhelmed by emotions." My mother looked at his hands—clasping a glass of bronze-colored liquid and ice. "OK. OK. I'm an emotional sort of guy."

The Professor writes me about hypernormalization, where people give up on the complex real world and build a fake world that they inhabit. Like Disney, like Vegas, like this place.

Zach was talking to me about U: "What I need is who she is."

U said to me, "I don't want to hear that kind of crap. I will tell you I'm exactly who he doesn't need."

U says, "They always want to look at you—but they never want to see you."

In the Ghost Lounge, I'm watching a cop show, figuring out if my alibi is as good as I think it is. Here are the clues: the terrible red tube of lipstick, the diffident wooden chair, the squat purple lamp. The TV remote with a broken button.

The woman seated next to me in the Team Session looks as if she has forgotten how to die. The sky is taped against the window.

We keep living until we don't know our lives anymore. Gravity situates itself around the TV—around the broken button on the TV remote.

P. A. Trick says, "That's why they don't put luggage racks on hearses."

In the community kitchen in our break room, Time crawls out of the silverware drawer.

WE CRASH INTO OUR GIANT
TIME-TELLING DEVICES

You believe you can carry around the
stars in a thimble. Always, time is thick
with what is around it. Time is the story
of our lives that vanishes as it is told.
Time is one event bumping into
another.
Koro Syndrome is when you believe
your penis has been stolen.
A virus has infected the system—trays
with piles of ash—strangled clocks—
blossoms crushed.
Empty space spills out of a tipped-over
thimble. Time is thick and gooey
and sticks to us—the way stars stick to
the darkness.

GOLDEN TOAD

"You know what this is like?" Wick says. "It's like waiting on a corner in a bombed village for an ice-cream truck. And that creepy, tinkly tune is playing over the ruins—coming closer and closer. Da da da dada da da dada da da da daaa." And Wick keeps humming the same tune over and over. Until we are all standing on that corner in that bombed-out village. And Stone, shaking his head, walks out with his clipboard and his report tucked under his arm.

see wick-apedia: Animal Language; Biosemiotics; Zoosemiotics.

Wick says, "I talk to animals. Really." P. A. Trick says she's a dream hacker—a shaman with a criminal's disposition. "Anyone can do it," says Wick. "Stop thinking. And, actually, stop talking."

"What are you talking about?" I ask.

"My mother was an alcoholic. And I'd hear all this howling and yelling and moaning around the house. That's when I learned how to talk to animals. But mostly the extinct ones."

She tells me, "In The Facility, a computer is thinking for us, but if you tell anyone they will call you crazy—and then they will send you somewhere else. I'm telling you because everyone already thinks you're crazy."

P. A. Trick is an aviatrix in the Pseudosphere—just buzzing around with blue hair—waiting to crash.

Because Stone (who despite all that's happened still asks us to call him Dr.) says we should, Wick and I both keep dream journals—then we start having each other's dreams. But it gets harder to tell what is the dream and what is the real. What is her dream and what is my reality?

Wick says it is like sleeping in a house on fire. She dwells in the center of erotic spirituality and the spiritually erotic. There is all this crazy around the color blue.

P. A. Trick says, "Wick as in Wick-an."

I hear the blood tick of the world's most ancient clock in the world's most absent animals.

PRAYER PUZZLES

The chapel in the madhouse
has a barbed wire cross. We need to
connect heaven and earth—through
Jacob's escalator.
Christ started stuffing light into the sack
of Lazarus's body. We want a shining
tomorrow that will eat the angry dark
message. It is almost like praying—
but praying for something bad to
happen on the altars made of beer cans
and hypodermic needles.
Jesus learned to breathe in the dirt.
Once Lazarus was brought back to life
he lived recklessly.
God was crazy. He talked crazy—with
his riddles, his inquisitions, his twilight
eyes, his brittle fingers. The wise men

mumbled so they could talk to God.
Crazy talk.
I am experiencing *susto*—I believe my
soul is gone.
Our prosthetic devices touch.
Now it is your turn: believe.
All around us, woven into the very
essence of creation, is the stunning
craziness of God.

DUSKY SEASIDE SPARROW

To Wick I say, "There's something galactic about you."

"Fuck off," she says.

"Yeah, like a black hole."

She likes that.

Wick says the universe was created by an advanced civilization for research purposes. Like The Facility. "Everything is lusciously fermentative, blindingly tragic. At one point, you just have to grab a broom."

P. A. Trick claims to be a victim of an excess amount of personality. "I've been molested by language. A pronoun isn't big enough to contain me."

The light is drizzly. Dream by dream. Drip by drop.

Wick says, "My father was in remission, but we didn't know from what."

The Professor once told me there was a man in the enlightenment who imagined a machine that could calculate the future. I look at the world coming toward me, and I try not to flinch.

P. A. Trick says, "Look at all the shit we try to sell each other. Shelves full of shiny shit. Aisles full of colossal shit. Shopping carts piled with polished shit. Half-price-off shit. Buy one pile of shit; get another pile of shit for free."

"If you want to have it done right, you've got to do it yourself,"

Zach said the day before he committed suicide. He created a machine that put an end to the future.

Wick and I are in the library with its pathetic self-help books. She pulls out a tattered book. "I never saw this one before," she says—and hands it to me. It is *The Myth of Sisyphus*. It looks like it has been scratched.

Zach used to tell me that God lives inside an Extinct Animal.

It probably goes without saying, but I'm not sure Wick is real.

SOMEONE I CALL I

Because I get tired of telling my story,
I start telling other people's stories.
Like the one that starts out
with someone I call *I*.
I can't figure out how to tell a story
that is about a journey inside a house—
that is about walking around inside the
different rooms.
I look up the words for crazy.
The trees lose the forest. The rivers lose
the fish. The characters inside the story
keep evaporating. The house begins to
eat its rooms.
The hunger inside the book is eating
the words, eating the darkness inside
the world that is made of stories.
The italicized *I* eats the other I.

SCIMITAR ORYX

I HOLD THE BOOK WICK HANDS ME. I see it perfectly now: this book takes its own life. I open it and see a hole burrowed deep inside it.

The walls are breathing in this tesseract house where P. A. Trick does his Thorazine shuffle to the Boobyhatch music he's humming—something he calls "Souliloque."

There will come a moment—an epicenter—from which all other moments emerge and return. A melting core. Slings and marrow—avatars of burned light in the museum of the future.

Wick says we are all part of a story told by an omniscient narrator with Alzheimer's. Stone asks the members of the Team Session, "Everyone go around the room and tell me who you are." I put my head down.

P. A. Trick says, "What are you doing? You can't brand a butterfly. You can't put goulashes on a swan."

At first, I was afraid of the dead body—as if I were responsible for it. And then it just seemed obvious: the body is me. But I cannot believe that. The moment is an egg where the bird lays ashes.

The dark is bite-out-of-the-middle-of-the-plum moist.

The Ink Keeper. The Beekeeper. The Be-ing Keeper. The Mind Keepers. The Story Keepers. They watch us do our waggle dances while they collect our honey.

The machinery inside the hive of the mind churns out a whole universe trembling in a shaky light.

This is when you are in love: when your heart is stapled to another heart—with that kind of destructive intimacy.

I hold up *The Myth of Sisyphus* and put my eye right up to the hole and read these words:

> There is no longer a single idea explaining everything, but an infinite number of essences giving a meaning to an infinite number of objects. The world comes to a stop, but also lights up.

Outside in the dark under the gazebo, the moon is nightly hatched.

TO WAKE UP THE SLEEPING MAP

THE SABRE-HORNED ANTELOPE (⅛ nat. size).

The eye scrapes over the earth.
Maps pulsate beneath the roads.
Micropsia is when objects appear
smaller than they actually are.
But, of course, everything is shrinking.
Pssst. Are there real people here?
Or is this just an elaborate confection?
The ventriloquist loses his words inside
the wooden mouth with the sawdust
and the splinters.
The first ever transmitted voice
message: "The horse does not eat
cucumber salad."
I measured mouths to make sure words
fit. They didn't. Eventually,
the horse did eat the cucumber salad.

HAWAIIAN CROW

STONE ASKS ME, "So which dreams are yours and which ones are Wick's?"

The dream about a burning train with faceless people waiting on the platform of the station. The dream about finding the hole where the river originates. These are Wick's.

The dream about God being a character in one of my dreams—where He is so self-absorbed. The dream about the ambulance that starts praying. The dream about a chorus line of dancers wearing gas masks. The dream about the dead balloonist floating over the hospital—throughout eternity. These are mine.

A weird sound comes from the basement like rain sprinkled on a thousand-stringed violin.

P. A. Trick says there is a method to their sadness. There are secret places in the blue heart where the snow doesn't stop falling.

Wick delights in the bee's multilingual labors.

There is a weird sound outside the windows like rain falling on a thousand open suitcases. U says Death tastes like Light.

I dream U tells me everything. Stone says now we are getting somewhere.

I admit it. I went into The Facility to make friends.

U tells me we live in the time of Betweens—ultimately

between our births and our deaths. Always we seem to be preoccupied with redemption. Sorry!

I tell U I dream there is a hole in the middle of a book, and I fall through it.

"I don't get it," I say to U. "You are saying there is no Zach. And if there is no Zach, then what about the suicide?" She looks over my shoulder at all of the Extinct Animals.

She stands in front of the elevator door, which doesn't open. She seems to stand there forever. "Between floors," she says.

TASTING THE LIGHT

The Photographer waits for the perfect
moment when she can taste the light,
and the moment lies naked before her.
The object hypnotizes the camera.
Our best view of the city came from the
top of the dump.
There are six kinds of sadness.
Number one: I push the fog in front of
me. Change happens when we forget
our fear.
Metanoia is the process of experiencing
a psychotic breakdown and subsequent
positive psychological healing.
Snap. Snap. There is a picture of us
crashing.

EASTERN COUGAR

I'M NOT SURE IF U IS FIRST THINKING WHAT I AM SAYING—or if I am saying what she is thinking. Either way we are saying each other's words. And I'm not too happy. Either way something has been stolen.

Wick opens up one of the thousand suitcases and finds one of her dreams inside it. The one where a bee flies out of her mouth.

At one time I wanted to be a Gnostic Alchemist, but there were no courses offered in it—except the one by the Professor. Thus, I began my intellectual-spiritual journey.

U tells me Professor Turritopsis Dohrnil is let go by the college. According to U, he is denied tenure because of "falsified documents." I am shocked. My mentor. My Dante Guide. My Untenured Guru. My Quantum Thinker.

The world is broken in too many places. We don't have enough stethoscopes to place on all of the brokennesses.

Professor Turritopsis Dohrnil: Cognoscente and Con; Wizard and Charlton; Guru and Quack; Shaman and Sham.

Wick says at night dreams eat you from the inside. There's a dream inside another dream—like a toybox, a toolbox, a text box. P. A. Trick says, "I'm a dart dipped in stardust." He hums "Rocket Man."

U asks, "Why do species go extinct?" Changes in climate, loss of habitat, pollution, hunting, invasive species, disease—all contributing factors. "OK. But what really happens is they run out of dreams—they run out of a reason to shuffle into the future."

P. A. Trick says, "Oh, gorgeous now here. I'm a diamond-headed drill. Who let the air out of the moon? Don't believe all the crap U tells you."

U hands me an envelope. It is a letter from Zach:

> Hope you've enjoyed my missives—my multiple mad-
> nesses—the Real After Party.

Wick tells me she will show me where time begins and takes me to the rose gazebo, where the bees fly around the blossoms in slow-motion blissfulness.

PHILOSOPHER OF ROTTING SHRINES

Are there dead people older than death?
The elders speak crazy stuff—goat-
brained—thought-choked.
I push the fog in front of me—a small
ticking time bomb is strapped to my
cerebellum.
I hear the drowning sounds
behind the trapdoors.
Capgras syndrome is when you believe
people you know have been replaced
by identical look-alikes.
Munching my way through worlds,
this is my impression of fading—
of seduction—of the color blue.
This is my impression of the bees, of the
gazebo, of the roses.

WESTERN BLACK RHINOCEROS

I DON'T GET IT. I fully believe that Lazarus would have been pissed. Wick tells me about the Potter Flower Bee. Extinct, of course.

Wick says she is going to have to leave soon. "You know, the astro-naught thing." She says dance is the essence of bee-ing. And she spells bee-ing to make sure I get it.

"Do you get it?" she asks.

Here's what I've learned from watching the bees around the rosebushes next to the gazebo:

Bees carry very tiny mirrors where they develop their craft— quaint and quixotic.

The bee translates the flower into its flying body.

Here's what I've learned from watching Wick: She holds a dictionary with a hole in the middle of it; this is where the words fall out.

The Extinct Animals whisper to everything that exists on the other side of the walls. They teach us to let go of the world. Those who have gone before us. It's OK, they say.

P. A. Trick calls it Infinite Luminosity. "The side effect of all the drugs I've ever been prescribed." P. A. Trick's fingers maneuver around a shuffled unopened deck.

Stone sits like he's waiting for Sisyphus. When you know everything is getting ready to be gone, you suddenly feel the slowing of time.

Wick says, "Can you hear it? The sound coming from the basement? The Infinite Luminosity?"

The Box I was carrying around was growing incredibly heavy. On the day Wick said she would be leaving soon, I decided to place the Box in the gazebo. The bees flew around it.

The world endlessly contorts itself into twisted shapes.

How many people does it take to finish the story?

I want to look into Wick's broken mirror and see everything.

THEY GROW TIRED OF DRINKING DEATH

In order to pay respect, taxidermists
wear entire birds on their heads.
Everything looks for home.
I take a bite out of the middle of time.
Fregoli syndrome is the delusional belief
that people you know are dressing up as
random people.
I keep seeing the same person
everywhere, and all of them are dressed
as birds.

HUMAN BEING

ON THE DAY SHE LEAVES, Wick leads me out to the gazebo in the courtyard; she says she'll show me where time comes from. And one of us laughs.

That's when I see the Potter Flower Bee stumble-flutter out of a rose.

Wick says, "In another life, I was a lover of Emily Dickinson. We are always in another life. Not physically lovers, of course. I would stand outside the gate of her house and attempt to whistle—though it sounded more like a siren in pain, or a train in a crash with something crushingly metallic."

I tell her that I understand. I write my autobiography in the plural.

I was afraid God would ask me to do something I didn't want to do—like kill a son or something. How do you respond to a request like that? Especially if you don't have a son.

In the lounge of The Facility, the TV screen comes to life—woozily, narcotically, aquatically. I hear the word, "Evanescence."

P. A. Trick moves on paws. "Get away from me," Trick says. Trick is in the Common Area playing Cosmic Chess—taking a piece from both sides—white pawn, black pawn, white knight, black queen—one at a time until the only thing left is the board—and then eventually the whole board evaporates—and everything experiences vacuum decay—a quantum bubble machine vaporizing everything it touches.

I bury my fear inside rain, so every time it rains, I tilt my head upward and let the fear soak my face in its deliciousness. Stone sits reading *The Myth of Sisyphus*.

I'm with Wick, and when the elevator door opens, there is a gazebo full of bees.

I bury the past in the future, so one day someone will stumble upon it with a shovel.

Wick says, "Bee! I'm expecting you!"

I bury my face in a broken mirror—so there are multiple faces. And all of them are me—and all of them are not me.

POTTER FLOWER FACILITY

CASE NUMBER

I'm not sure exactly what happened.

That night I had a dream. There was a lake full of floating heads—sharing secrets. It wasn't creepy. It wasn't scary. It was quiet and mysterious and somehow comforting. All the Extinct Animals were among the floating heads.

There are only two options: either we die or we tell stories.

SYMPTOMS

Wick left behind a suitcase, and when I opened it, I found the Self-Portrait, the Mind Map, and the List of Contents.

There was a slip of paper.

U had written: One day there will be a great vanishing.

PSYCHOSOCIAL HISTORY

Time fell out of the gazebo.

Wick becomes me and I become her. I guess I always knew it. Of course, we eventually become the bee.

Sometimes words don't fit in the mouth, and there's no room left

for the tongue. I carry time on my back, and we pretend we are
alive.

TREATMENT HISTORY

That night I had a dream. There is a lake full of floating heads—
sharing secrets. Unblinking. Tranquil under the moon. Stone is
among the floating heads. And the Professor. And P. A. Trick. And
U. And Wick.

And in the middle of the lake, Zach is fishing. So mesmerizingly
peaceful. Nothing can disturb the surface of the world around him.

Under the torn button of the moon, Zach sits in his rowboat. Out
in the middle of the lake, nothing disturbs the surface of the world
around him.